Augie to Zebra

An Alphabet Book!

Kate Endle &
Caspar Babypants

SASQUATCH BOOKS
SEATTLE

Aa

Augie
Awards the
Ape

Bb

Bella
Becomes the
Butterfly

Cc

Carmin
Cradles
Cats

Dd

Darla
Draws
Dogs

Ee

Eliza
Educates the
Elephant

Ff

Frederico
Follows
Frogs

Gg

Gabby
Grooms
Geese

Hh

Hiroshi Hugs the Hippo

Ii

Ivan Invites the Iguana

To: ♥ Iguana

INK

Jj

Josie
Jams with
Jaguars

Kk

Komiko
Kicks with the
Kangaroo

Ll

Levi
Looks at
Ladybugs

Mm

Manny's in the
Middle of
Monkeys

Nn Nalani Naps with Nuthatches

Oliver

Organizes

Owls

Pp

Pasquale Paints with the Panda

Qq

Quinn
Quiets
Quails

Rr

Ricardo
Reads to
Raccoons

Ss

Sisika
Sings with
Sparrows

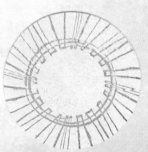

Tt Tamekah Tickles the Tiger

U u

Umberto
Unites
Unicorns

Vv Viola
Vaults over
Vultures

Ww

Willy
Washes the
Walrus

Xx

Xavier eXamines the Xeme

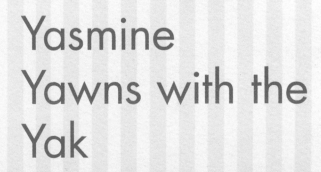

Yy

Yasmine
Yawns with the
Yak

Zz

Zara
Zooms with the
Zebra

CAN YOU FIND THESE OTHER ITEMS THAT START WITH EACH LETTER?

A apple, ant, acorn, arrow
B ballet shoes, blue, black, barrette, buttons
C chair, cap, cuddling, carpet
D denim, daisies, dachsund, drawings
E eagle, egg, easel, ear, eraser
F fly, face, feet, fingers, flowers, fence, ferns
G girl, green, geraniums, grass, goslings
H hat, hands, happy, happy birthday, heart
I ice, invitation, ivy, inside, indigo
J jackets, jeans, jug, jester, jungle, jump
K kimono, kingfisher, kettle, knee, koala bear
L lantern, legs, log, leaf, labrador, lunch box
M mad, mask, melon, maracas
N noon, notebook, notes, nuts, nest
O orange, overcoat, owlets, oak leaf, okay
P painting, purple, pink, parrot, plaid pants
Q quilt, quill pen, queen
R rocket, red, rug, radio, robot, rocking horse
S sailboat, sun, sandwich, strawberries, swing
T trees, tail, t-shirt, tummy, teeth, toucan
U umbrella, unicycle, underpants, ukulele
V violets (flowers), violet (color), vest, vines
W watering can, washcloth, wagon, whiskers
X xenops, x-ray, xylophone
Y yarn, yellow jacket, yams, yo-yo
Z zinnias, zigzag, zipper, zoo

KATE ENDLE grew up in Northeast Ohio and attended the Columbus College of Art and Design. Her illustrations can be found in magazines, greeting cards, children's books, and home decor products. With scissors, acrylic medium, and a wide selection of hand-painted and decorative papers, she created another avenue for her love of design and color. Find out more at KateEndle.com. She lives in Seattle with her husband Chris Ballew.

CASPAR BABYPANTS is also known as Chris Ballew, twice Grammy-nominated lead singer and songwriter for the rock-and-roll band The Presidents of the United States of America. After years of tinkering with simple innocent tunes, Chris rediscovered folk and traditional music and focused his songwriting for kids, which gave birth to Caspar Babypants. Find out more at BabypantsMusic.com. He lives in Seattle.

Manufactured in China by C&C Offset Printing Co. Ltd. Shenzhen, Guangdong Province, in February 2012

Published by Sasquatch Books
17 16 15 14 13 12   9 8 7 6 5 4 3 2 1

Cover and interior illustrations and layout: Kate Endle
Book Composition: Rebecca Shapiro/Sarah Plein
Library of Congress Cataloging-in-Publication Data is available.

ISBN-13: 978-1-57061-750-8
ISBN-10: 1-57061-750-3

Sasquatch Books
1904 Third Avenue, Suite 710
Seattle, WA 98101
(206) 467-4300
www.sasquatchbooks.com
custserv@sasquatchbooks.com